KU-467-545

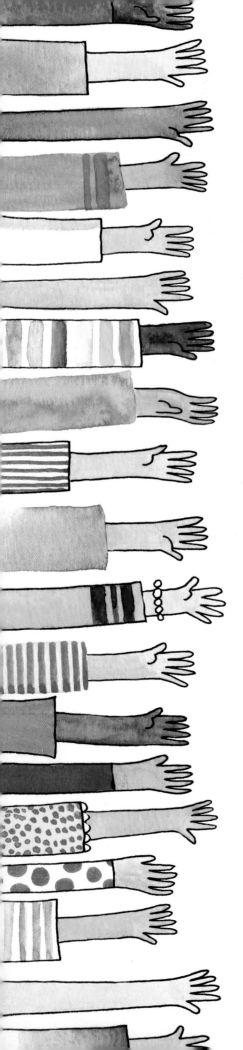

For my mom

BRENT LIBRARIES	
KIN	
91120000426813	
Askews & Holts	07-Feb-2020
JF	£6.99

ABOUT THIS BOOK

The illustrations for this book were created using watercolor, colored pencil, and ink, then were digitally finished. This book was edited by Kheryn Callender and designed by Jamie W. Yee with art direction by Saho Fujii. The production was supervised by Erika Schwartz, and the production editor was Marisa Finkelstein. The text was set in HighlanderITC, and the display type is Zemke Hand ITC.

Copyright © 2018 by Sharee Miller • Cover illustration copyright © 2018 by Sharee Miller • Cover design by Jamie W. Yee. • Cover copyright © 2018 by Hachette Book Group, Inc. • Hachette Book Group supports the right to free expression and the value of copyright. The purpose of copyright is to encourage writers and artists to produce the creative works that enrich our culture. • The scanning, uploading, and distribution of this book without permission is a theft of the author's intellectual property. If you would like permission to use material from the book (other than for review purposes), please contact permissions@hbgusa.com. Thank you for your support of the author's rights. • Little, Brown and Company • Hachette Book Group • 1290 Avenue of the Americas, New York, NY 10104 • Visit us at LBYR.com • Originally published in hardcover and ebook by Little, Brown and Company in November 2018 • First Trade Paperback Edition: November 2019 • Little, Brown and Company is a division of Hachette Book Group, Inc. • The Little, Brown name and logo are trademarks of Hachette Book Group, Inc. • The publisher is not responsible for websites (or their content) that are not owned by the publisher. • The Library of Congress has cataloged the hardcover edition as follows: Names: Miller, Sharee (Illustrator), author, illustrator. • Title: Don't touch my hair! / Sharee Miller. • Other titles: Do not touch my hair! • Description: First edition. | New York : Little, Brown and Company, 2018. | Summary: Aria loves her soft and bouncy hair, but must go to extremes to avoid people who touch it without permission until, finally, she speaks up. Includes author's note. • Identifiers: LCCN 2017044073 | ISBN 9780316562584 (hardcover) | ISBN 9780316484084 (ebook) | ISBN 9780316522427 (library edition ebook) • Subjects: | CYAC: Hair—Fiction. | Assertiveness (Psychology)—Fiction. | African Americans—Fiction. • Classification: LCC PZ7. M6336 Don 2018 | DDC [E]—dc23 • LC record available at https://lccn.loc.gov/2017044073 • ISBNs: 978-0-316-56257-7 (pbk.), 978-0-316-48408-4 (ebook), 978-0-316-48410-7 (ebook), 978-0-316-48409-1 (ebook) • PRINTED IN CHINA • 1010 • 10 9 8 7 6 5 4 3 2 1

DON'T TOUCH MY HAIR!

SHAREE MILLER

LB

LITTLE, BROWN AND COMPANY

NEW YORK BOSTON

I'm Aria, and this is my hair.

I love my hair. It's soft and bouncy, and grows up toward the sun like a flower.

I love it up or down.

Styled or wild, I don't care!
I just want it to be free.

It's great that people love my hair, but some love it so much they want to touch it! I don't like this.

They are so curious about my hair that they try to touch it without even asking for permission!

I get very good at avoiding hands.

I have to start looking
for ways to hide my hair.

I try blending in with the scenery...
but I'm quickly spotted.

I try hiding underwater, but that doesn't last long.

I escape to the jungle,
but the critters just can't
keep their hands to
themselves!

Even in the tallest castle tower, someone is always there, ready and waiting to touch my hair.

No matter how far I go, it doesn't seem to matter.

Finally, I find a place where
no one wants to touch my hair...
but after a few hours, I get lonely.

I decide to go home.

I try my best to ignore the attention.
But as a hand sinks into my hair...

The next time someone wants to touch my hair, they ask,

Now it feels great to walk down the street without anyone trying to touch my hair. My curls are free to reach for the sun, just like a flower.

Some people still ask to touch my hair, but if I say no, they listen.

But if you ask nicely,
sometimes I say,

AUTHOR'S NOTE

I started this book a few years ago, based on my own experiences—though monkeys, mermaids, dragons, and aliens have never tried to touch my hair, other human beings have!

Many people often feel uncomfortable or disrespected when others touch their hair without permission. Though Aria struggles specifically with people touching her hair in this book, this is also a story about personal boundaries and what I would like to be used as a tool to teach the importance of asking for permission first. I hope that, after reading *Don't Touch My Hair!*, children can learn the importance of asking for permission and of not being afraid to say "no"—and not being afraid to hear "no," too!

When creating the art, I used bright colors to match the humor of the text. I used colored pencil for Aria's hair so it would have texture and stand out from the rest of the art in the book.

Author photo © Darrell Hanley

SHAREE MILLER has a BFA in communication design from Pratt Institute. She lives in Brooklyn, where she enjoys spending time with her two cats and illustrating fun stories. Sharee invites you to visit her website at shareemiller.com and her Instagram @coilyandcute.